About the Author

Lin Palmer is Plymouth born and bred, a Plymouth maid.
She lives in Plymouth with her husband, son and daughter
and enjoys walking on Dartmoor with their three dogs.

To

Lesley,

Best Wishes,

Lin
Palmer

Dedication

For my son James and daughter Char.

Thank you Char for the brilliant illustrations.

And finally in memory of my lovely mum who always believed in me.

By Lin Palmer
Illustrated by Char Palmer

PLYMOUTH MAID

AUSTIN MACAULEY
PUBLISHERS LTD.

A CIP catalogue record for this title is available from the British Library.

ISBN 9781785541650 (Paperback)
ISBN 9781785541667 (Hardback)
ISBN 9781785541674 (E-Book)

www.austinmacauley.com

First Published (2016)
Austin Macauley Publishers Ltd.
25 Canada Square
Canary Wharf
London
E14 5LQ

Acknowledgments

I would like to thank my daughter Char for doing the illustrations.

Contents

A BIRTHDAY EXCUSE	15
A DANGEROUS EXERCISE	16
A DOG IS FOR LIFE	17
A FARMER'S PROBLEM	18
A SHORT ODE	19
A THANK YOU FROM JAMES	20
A TRIBUTE TO A VERY SPECIAL LADY - OUR MUM, 2009	21
A VALENTINE WISH	22
BABYS' DAY OUT	23
BIRTHDAY CANDLE WARNING FOR AGES 40 AND OVER	24
BORN TO RUN FREE - A TRIBUTE TO RESCUE CENTRES	25
BOUNCER AND THE WALL	26
BROKEN DOWN AGAIN	27
CARAVANNING	29
CHASING MARINES	30
CHEWING GUM - A MESSAGE FROM OUR DOG ZAC	32
DO YOU REMEMBER	33
DOES THE WASHING MACHINE EAT MY SOCKS?	34
DON'T LET THE DOG OUT	35
DON'T LOOK AT ME IN THAT TONE OF VOICE	36
DON'T MAKE ME GO TO SCHOOL MUM	37
DON'T OPEN THE DRIVER'S SIDE WINDOW	38
ENERGY DRINKS, MY REPLY TO A TEACHER'S LETTERS	40
FREEDOM IS (A POEM DONE TOGETHER WITH DAUGHTER CHARLOTTE FOR A PRIMARY SCHOOL PROJECT IN 2009)	41
GERMAN SHEPHERD WALKING IN THE RAIN	42
GLASSES	44
HELP...I'M LOCKED IN MY CAR	45
HOW CAN I MISS YOU (IF YOU WON'T GO AWAY)?	46

IN MEMORY OF MY BEST FRIEND SCAMP 48
IT CAN ONLY HAPPEN TO ME 49
IT DOESN'T SNOW IN PLYMOUTH (VERY OFTEN) 50
IT TOWS SO FINE 51
LOCKED OUT 52
ME GARDEN'S UNDER WATER! 53
MOONLIGHT BECOMES YOU? 54
MOUSE 55
MY CAMERA 56
MY CARAVAN IS LEAKING 57
MY DANGEROUS DAUGHTER CHARLOTTE 58
WHERE'S ME TENT 59
MY HERO 61
MY LITTLE CAR IS PAST IT! 62
MY PASSPORT NEEDS RENEWING 64
NOSEY NEIGHBOUR 66
ODE TO A LAND ROVER 67
OFF TO DARTMOOR 68
OFF TO UNI (A LITTLE MESSAGE FOR MUM) 69
OH DEER IT'S MARK 70
OH HECK - ME BRAKES HAVE FAILED 71
OLD FLAME I DON'T THINK SO 73
AN EXPENSIVE WALK 74
ONLY A DOG 75
OUCH ME HEAD 76
OUR PUPPY 77
OUR PUPPY LOKI 78
OUR ZAC 79
PLEASE CAN I HAVE MY BABY BACK 80
PLEASE TELL ME GOODBYE 81
POOR DOG 82
PUTTING UP THE AWNING 83
RAIN 84
SANTA'S JOKE 85
SCARY! 86
SID THE SPIDER 87
THAT RUDDY G.P.S 88
THE BEACH WALK 89
THE BROKEN DOWN LAND ROVER 90
THE CAT 92

THE COMPANY MAN 93
THE DIRTY DOG 94
THE DOG'S THOUGHTS 95
THE DRUNK 96
THERE'S SLUGS IN ME GARDEN 97
THE EXAM 99
THE FAULTY CAR ALARM 100
THE FEMALE DRUNK 102
DEDICATED TO JACKS BRANCH FREDDIE – OUR
GREYHOUND 2003 to 2008 103
THE GUY SINGING TWO FIELDS AWAY 104
THE HEDGEHOG 106
THE DOG 107
THE OWL 108
THE PASSING OF NORMAN THE GOLDFISH 109
THE PLOT 110
THE PUPPY IN THE BATH 111
THE RETIREMENT POEM 112
THE ROBIN 113
THE SCHOOL RUN 114
THE WASHING MACHINE 116
THERE'S A RAT IN ME OUTHOUSE! 117
THOSE BLINKING CHRISTMAS LIGHTS 118
THOUGHTS OF OUR GERMAN SHEPHERD AT THE
VETS! 119
THOUGHTS OF AN OLD AGED POP STAR 121
WE DON'T WANT OUR PHOTO TAKEN MUM 122
WHAT A RACKET 123
WHERE DID I PARK MY CAR 124
WHERE'S ME CHRISTMAS TURKEY 125
WHY ARE MY TEENAGERS ALLERGIC TO THE BIN 126
WRONG NUMBER 127

A BIRTHDAY EXCUSE

I am so very sorry, that you didn't get a card from me.
To celebrate your special day, but, I'll explain you see…

I was held hostage, by my big black GSD,
He wouldn't let me post your card,
He wouldn't set me free.

I couldn't get out the front door,
I couldn't get out the back,
I couldn't just creep past him,
That GSD called Zac.

I couldn't leave in daylight,
I couldn't leave in dark,
Cos each time that I tried it,
That flipping dog would bark.

I couldn't take him with me,
To the corner of our street,
As if he saw another dog,
He'd drag me off my feet.

Happy Birthday anyway,
I hope your day was great,
This was really an excuse,
Because my card is late!

A DANGEROUS EXERCISE

Well, I did me exercises, when I finished doing ten,
I went to get up off the floor, but couldn't get up again.

I crawled along the carpet, I just couldn't get upright,
So I grabbed hold of the nearest chair, as I couldn't stay there
all night.

I pulled myself into the chair, and here is where I sit,
I no longer worry, whether I am fit.

So sod the exercises, and those urges to get fit,
I think that in the future, I'll just sit here and knit!

A DOG IS FOR LIFE

I'm very sad and lonely, I'm tired and hungry too,
I'd really love a caring home, can I come home with you?

I used to have a home once, when I was just a pup,
But the children there who owned me, started to grow up.

They wanted latest fashions, and things in shops they see,
They really can't be bothered, with such a dog as me.

I really need some shelter now, my pups are nearly due,
I'm getting really worried, oh what am I to do.

I wake up very suddenly, I've been asleep a week,
A kindly voice just spoke to me, it made me want to weep.

My puppies have been born now, four, or so they said,
I heard them whisper there were six, but sadly two are dead.

I know that I am safe here, there's kindness all around,
I'm told I'm in a shelter, not in a doggy pound.

The people, they are kind here, I do not have to roam,
I'm no longer cold and hungry, as I've been found a home.

A FARMER'S PROBLEM

I have a problem, which just won't keep,
My sheepdog is afraid of sheep.

I bought him as a little pup,
His dad for rounding, won a cup.

But this dog, when put near sheep,
Out of his skin, he does near leap.

The sheep they do think this is fun,
And straight at him, they always run.

Now I am just a farming bloke,
But rounding sheep, I'm now a joke.

The only way I'll win the cup,
Is to train another pup.

One thing's for sure, if he can't sleep,
My dog he won't be counting sheep!

A SHORT ODE

There's nothing on the T.V. tonight,
It seems we're out of luck,
So I've given up and turned it off,
I think I'll read me book!

A THANK YOU FROM JAMES

Just a gift from me to you,
As I move on to pastures new.

Thanking you for all you've done,
I know it wasn't always fun.

And as I start my new college in September,
It'll be you that I'll always remember.

No more of our fun and games,
This comes with love from your friend James.

A TRIBUTE TO A VERY SPECIAL LADY - OUR MUM, 2009

What will we do without you Mum,
We don't know what to say.
What will we do without your love,
As we carry on each day.

We miss your smile, we miss your voice,
The funny things you do,
What will we do without you Gran,
We miss you dearly too.

What do we do without you Mum?
We know we had to part,
But you will never leave us Mum,
We have you in our hearts.

A VALENTINE WISH

Please come and visit me,
Or just drop me a line,
I've written this poem just for you,
I wish that you were mine.

I'd really love to meet you,
I wish we could be friends,
But you don't know that I exist,
And so my story ends.

I really wish you'd contact me,
I think you're really nice,
I really want to be your friend,
It would be very nice.

We would make a good team,
If only we could get together,
And it would be just fine,
If you would stay forever.

But this isn't gonna happen,
Life to me is mean,
This little chance of happiness,
Is only just a dream.

BABYS' DAY OUT

We went for a visit as families do,
Taking our children to visit the zoo.

Birds and reptiles, mammals big and small,
We looked in their cages, and visited them all.

Lots of creatures, and so much to do,
The world seems so big, when you're only aged two!

BIRTHDAY CANDLE WARNING
FOR AGES 40 AND OVER

As you light your candles,
on your birthday cake,
Don't do it in the house,
as the heat it just won't take.

Happy birthday my friend,
Hope your day is fun,
If you're asked how old you are,
tell 'em twenty-one!

Hope that your party,
Goes off like it should,
And that your special day,
Is really very good!

BORN TO RUN FREE - A TRIBUTE
TO RESCUE CENTRES

The Greyhound they say, was born to run,
But not on a track, it should be for fun.

Please note these dear dogs, have beauty and grace,
Not meant for a track, where they're then forced to race.

They're not, unwanted items, to be just thrown away,
When their races are lost at the end of the day.

They too have feelings, and trust you to do right,
Not dump them on motorways in the dead of the night.

We own an ex racer, and say Thanks a bunch,
For saving our best friend, whose name was 'Quick Lunch'

Now when he's racing, this dog you do see,
It's for winning first place on the front room's settee!

BOUNCER AND THE WALL

This isn't really funny at all,
My dog he jumped the neighbour's wall.
I'd only popped out to the shop,
And over the wall, my dog did hop.

I stand in shock, let out a sigh,
Can't climb that wall, it's much too high.
Even their gate at me it mocked,
Always open, today it's locked.

My neighbour, she has gone to work,
That dog of mine is such a burke,
It isn't any good at all,
As I try to get him to jump the wall.

And so I decide to have a go,
I grab his paw and start to pull.
A paw then two, I catch hold tight,
And pull him back with all my might.

At last I cheer, I've got you free,
Now back in the garden,
Here with me.

That prank you pulled,
Was not very funny,
As our neighbour now has,
A very shocked bunny!

BROKEN DOWN AGAIN

I'm sure my car is out to get me,
It wants to do me harm,
'cos after we had had our walk,
I couldn't turn off the alarm.

I only flicked the button, to open up the car,
But it started the alarm off, so I knew I couldn't drive far.
On and on and on it went, it filled me full of woe,
And then to start the car up, and finding it won't go.

So there I am just stranded, I am there alone,
So I reach into my pocket, and then pull out my phone.
I'm getting very well known, to the Breakdown Company,
All I have to say now is…Hello again, it's me!

I explain the situation, and give directions where we are,
But really he could follow, the noise coming from my car.
My German Shepherd he starts barking, as a stranger he can see.
He makes more noise than the alarm, as he's protecting me.

Still the alarm goes on and on, will it ever stop,
The guy parks up his breakdown truck, and out the cab he hops.
He pulls out the alarm thing, and sticks it in the ground.
And finally the flipping thing, stops making that awful sound!

It takes a really long time, but we still cannot go afar,
'cos I really need the garage, to fix my little car.

As he couldn't really fix it, it really was quite dire,
But at least I do know now,
How my car I can hot wire!

CARAVANNING

Holding up the traffic,
Making them go slow,
Towing with my caravan,
As on holiday I go.

Putting up the awning,
In the pouring rain,
It happened to us last time,
It's happening again.

The wind it is a howling,
As on the site we stay,
I'm glad we have our caravan,
As the tents have blown away.

When the weather does turn nicer,
A BBQ's just right.
With lights around our awning,
It looks pretty late at night.

Now the holiday is over,
Back on the road we go,
Travelling to our storage site,
With the caravan in tow.

CHASING MARINES

Walking on the Moors the dogs and I,
When out of the gorse, my dog Zac does spy.

Various guys in browns and greens,
Running along, it was the Marines.

Zac he watched them on their run,
And thought, oh boy, this could be fun.

I felt his lead jerk in my hand,
He wanted to join this running band,

Of men dressed in brown and green,
He wanted to catch himself a Marine!

Now over the Moors, it 'ain't much fun,
Chasing Marines in the blazing sun.

You may just think it's such a blast,
But these Marines, they run too fast.

Although to Zac, not quite a blow,
As he found a couple, who were going slow.

Carrying lots of heavy kit,
These Marines weren't quite as fit.

So Ladies, if a Marine's your taste,
And you'll settle for one with a slower pace.

I'll give you my number, so you can get back,
And place your order with my dog Zac!

CHEWING GUM - A MESSAGE FROM OUR DOG ZAC

Do not stick your gum in any place but the bin,
Don't drop it in Zac's bed as it's what he sleeps in.

He's getting rather fed up, as it's sticky and it's sweet,
And it sticks like glue upon his fur and the pads upon his feet.

A black German Shepherd dog, chewing on some gum,
Or blowing bubbles with it, might just look like fun.

But Zac would like to point out that his fur it does get stuck,
And he doesn't like gum anyway, in fact he thinks it's yuck!

DO YOU REMEMBER

Do you remember being young,
And those long hot summer days?

Do you remember when you went to school,
And all the friends you made?

Do you remember the then pop stars?
I could but name a few, Donny Osmond, David Cassidy and
the Partridge family too.

Were you a teenager in nineteen seventy?
If you were, then you will be, the very same age as me!

DOES THE WASHING MACHINE EAT MY SOCKS?

Does the washing machine eat my socks? I don't know what they do,
'cos when I take them out of there.
There's one instead of two.

Now, I find that this very odd,
Where have they gone I beg,
If I'm lucky, I'll take out three,
Who has an extra leg!

The washing machine has stopped now,
At me it daily mocks,
If it carries much longer,
Then I'll run out of socks!

DON'T LET THE DOG OUT

Don't let the dog out into the garden,
I know he wants to go,
But once he gets outside the house,
He'll start to dig a hole.

He's already trashed the flower bulbs,
They flew across the mud.
I knew exactly what he'd done,
When they hit me with a thud.

Not satisfied his work was done,
He wanted to impress,
And so another hole's appeared,
He didn't half make a mess.

But, I don't mind him digging,
It depends on where he'll go.
He dug one on the path last night,
And I fell down that hole.

Now I watch him from the window,
He is causing more disaster,
And after falling down that pit,
My foot is now in plaster!

DON'T LOOK AT ME IN THAT TONE OF VOICE

Don't look at me, in that tone of voice,
You've been glaring at me all day.
I don't know if I've upset you,
I haven't heard you say.

If looks could kill, I'd be a goner,
You look at me with spite,
Don't look at me in that tone of voice,
Haven't I done something right.

Don't look at me in that tone of voice,
You'll have me run a mile,
I don't know what looks worse now,
As you look at me and smile.

DON'T MAKE ME GO TO SCHOOL MUM

Don't make me go to school Mum,
As I don't like it there,
All the teachers hate me,
And I don't think that it's fair.

Don't make me go to school Mum,
The students think I'm thick,
Can't you ring them up Mum,
And tell them I am sick.

Don't make me go to school Mum,
I just don't like the Head,
It would be so nice Mum,
If I could stay in bed.

I think you're really mean Mum,
You just stand there and laugh,
What's that, that you said Mum,
I must go, 'cos I'm Staff!

DON'T OPEN THE DRIVER'S SIDE WINDOW

Don't open the driver's side window,
If you do then it will stick,
Don't open the driver's side window,
As the electrics they are sick.

If you open the driver's side window,
You'll be out of luck,
'cos it will never close again,
It's well and truly stuck.

Don't open the driver's side window,
The car is getting old,
And once the windows open wide,
You'll get good and cold.

Now, I'm fed up with this window,
It really is a pain,
I opened it as I forgot,
And me seat is full of rain.

So, don't open the driver's side window,
Until it is the spring,
As it is that much warmer then,
And you'll hear the birdies sing.

Don't open the driver's side window please,
As the wind does coldly blow,
And as this car is driving me mad,
It's time for it to go.

ENERGY DRINKS, MY REPLY TO A TEACHER'S LETTERS

Put down those energy drinks kids,
I won't have them in my school,
They make you more unruly,
And the teachers look a fool.

If you bring in those energy drinks kids,
I will confiscate them,
I will not give them back,
'cos I really, really hate them.

Get rid of those energy drinks kids,
I've written letters home,
I know you've told your parents,
The old codgers having a moan.

Leave home those energy drinks kids,
Now I'm getting so annoyed,
I know that you are laughing,
As you think I'm paranoid.

I've banned those energy drinks kids,
WHAT! They must be having a laugh,
I walked into the staff room,
they're being drunk now by the staff!

FREEDOM IS (A POEM DONE TOGETHER WITH DAUGHTER CHARLOTTE FOR A PRIMARY SCHOOL PROJECT IN 2009)

The sun on my face, the wind in my hair,
Family and friends, people who care.

To be able to speak without terror or fear,
Or being imprisoned or just disappear.

No hatred, no violence, no wars, all would cease,
A world full of freedom, freedom and peace.

GERMAN SHEPHERD WALKING IN THE RAIN

Oh why won't my GSD go out walking in the rain.
I try to take him with me, but it really is a pain.

A dog as big as he is, should like to walk afar.
But when the rain begins to fall, he won't get out of the car.

I push him and I pull him, it really is a sight,
As he backs further into the car putting up a fight.

He really should enjoy a walk, on the Moors so free.
But instead he's in the dry, and in the wet is me.

The rain comes down so heavily, I give him one last pull,
And as he's not expecting it, from the car he has to go.

We finally get started, on our walk so muddy and wet,
He has a sniff around the ground, but hasn't finished yet.

Then as we turn the corner, and the car he now has 'see'd'.
Knowing that he'll soon be dry, we set off at some speed.

Now, walking on wet moorland, is not a perfect trip,
And over mud and water, I soon begin to slip.

Getting closer to my car, he now makes one last dash,
And I end up outside my door, sitting on the grass.

My GSD is happy now, he's no longer filled with sorrow,
The whole thing will then start again, when we come back
tomorrow.

GLASSES

Oh, I hate me glasses, they keep running away,
No matter when I leave them, they just don't seem to stay.

I need them for reading, as I just cannot see,
The small print without them, means nothing there to me.

The places that they get to, my memory it does jog,
In fact, there was this one time, they got sat on by my dog.

At last now I can keep them, oh, what a wonderful thing,
So on my neck I place them, hanging from a string.

HELP...I'M LOCKED IN MY CAR

I got locked in me car,
'Twas on the Monday morning,
It happened very quickly,
I didn't get a warning.

I'd pulled into the car park,
But I then started to doubt,
As I tried the door handle,
And it wouldn't let me out.

No opening of the front doors,
As there certainly is a lack,
And so now being desperate,
I climbed into the back.

Getting in there safely,
Is really quite a feat,
As I now have to climb over,
The very high front seat.

I try the other doors then,
And I am filled with glee,
As the back ones, they do open,
And at last then I am free.

Now, no more with the doors,
Do I have to fight,
As it's gone off to the garage,
And they have put it right.

HOW CAN I MISS YOU (IF YOU WON'T GO AWAY)?

The house wasn't empty, when I came home today,
Tell me, how can I miss you, if you won't go away.

I'd like to say I'm sorry, and ask you please to stay,
But how can I miss you if you won't go away.

In the bedroom this morning, I looked upon the bed,
Instead of being empty, on the pillow lies your head,

Please can you tell me, why it is you stay,
How can I miss you, if you won't go away?

I so want you to leave me, but I can't get you to go,
So once again I ask you, just so as I will know,

How can I miss you, if you won't go away?

Why can't you take a gentle hint, leave me, say Goodbye.
I promise I won't get upset, I won't even cry.

Tell me please, I need to know why you didn't leave today,
How can I miss you, if you won't go away?

You tell me, you won't ever leave,
Will never say Goodbye,
My eyes they start welling up,
I think I'm gonna cry.

I can't understand it,
I ask you every day,
How can I miss you,
when you just won't GO AWAY!

IN MEMORY OF MY BEST FRIEND
SCAMP

Please excuse me while I weep,
For my best friend who went to sleep.
Near thirteen years we've been together,
I thought that time would last forever.

But age is something we all do,
and though I thought the world of you,
I had to do what was right, with tears in my eyes, I whisper
"Goodnight"

You were my dog, I loved you so,
With a broken heart I let you go,
To a place with no more pain,
And you are once more young again.

Please excuse me while I weep,
For my best friend who I can't keep,
But there lies within my heart,
Memories of you, we'll never part.

IT CAN ONLY HAPPEN TO ME

Why is it that when anything happens,
Tell me, as I just can't see,
that whatever or wherever it happens,
It can only happen to me?

Why when things go from bad to worse,
And with other people I'll be,
The things that then do happen,
They will only happen to me?

So if we go out together,
and things just don't go right,
You don't have to worry, about the things that may or might,
whatever then will happen, what will be will be,
As whatever the problem is, it will only happen to me.

IT DOESN'T SNOW IN PLYMOUTH (VERY OFTEN)

It doesn't snow in Plymouth,
It really is quite boring,
Whilst everywhere else has snow,
In Plymouth it is pouring.

Why can't we be like Switzerland, or Austria with snow,
You don't get that in Plymouth,
Because it just 'ain't so.

It doesn't snow in Plymouth,
In winter it just rains,
In Plymouth we getting flooding,
As the leaves block up the drains.

IT TOWS SO FINE

I bought a caravan, I hope to tow behind,
My little jeep, when the sun does shine.
We'll travel up and down the roads some time,
Because it's mine, it tows so fine.

When the sun shines and the weekend's here,
I load the 'van up with all my camping gear,
To the campsite with friends from far and near.
I think it's fine, this 'van of mine.

There's entertainment on the Saturday night,
We join in singing late into the night,
We could stay and sing along all night,
But as it's nine, we watch the time.

And finally, now that Sunday's here,
After flagpole, we pack up all our gear,
And wave to friends, who call, see you next year.
A wonderful time, with friends of mine.

So, back there on the road we go,
Our little van behind us which we tow,
Sad to leave the rally field behind,
It was so fine, what a lovely time.

LOCKED OUT

It's just not fair, oh woe is me,
I went out and shut my door,
That was a silly thing to do,
As I can't get in no more.

I didn't realise what I'd done,
Leaving behind my key,
It is locked within my house,
And outside there stands me.

When at last I get inside,
I decided what I will do,
Next time instead of one key,
I'll make sure I carry two.

ME GARDEN'S UNDER WATER!

I look out of my window,
As things ain't as they oughta,
And I can't see me garden,
As it's three feet under water.

The rain it keeps on pouring,
I give a little shiver,
Just now I had a puddle,
But now I have a river!

My grass, it had grown quite high,
I said I need a goat,
But now, what I really need,
Is a lifeguard and a boat!

MOONLIGHT BECOMES YOU?

Moonlight flatters you,
It makes you look good.
This really surprises me,
As nothing else could!

Moonlight becomes you,
Or that's what they say.
They obviously haven't met you,
Or they scream and run away.

Moonlight becomes you,
But total darkness suits you better,
Think that I'm joking?
Just wait until you've met her!

MOUSE

I went into the kitchen,
To make a cup of tea,
And saw it dart across the floor,
I wondered, did I see...

I looked around the floor then,
Was it all a dream,
But then it ran between my legs,
And I gave out a scream.

I don't know how it got there,
Running through my house,
But next door's cat just caught it,
Yes, it was a mouse.

MY CAMERA

I own a brand new camera,
It cost me quite a lot,
It really is so special,
And it takes a brilliant shot.

It's better than some other makes,
For that you can be sure,
I wouldn't have a different one,
Coming in my door.

My camera is quite wonderful,
This camera is quite fine,
With all its little gadgets,
I'm glad that it is mine.

There is one little problem though,
I really had a shock,
didn't turn the flash on right,
So no photos I have got.

So just a word of warning,
If you're posing with your gear,
And you want to take the mickey,
Out of stuff that's not so dear,

It's not just the equipment,
That gets the shot in sight,
'tis the one behind the camera,
Who makes sure things is right!

MY CARAVAN IS LEAKING

My caravan is leaking,
The walls are sopping wet,
Now it's dripping from the ceiling,
I haven't stopped it yet.

It's driving me real crazy,
I can't get it to dry,
No matter what I do,
No matter how I try.

The rain it is a pouring,
It's making things seem so bad,
I gaze upon my leaky 'van,
It makes me feel quite sad.

Maybe there is a bright side,
As things they look so dire,
With all the wet inside my 'van,
At least it won't catch fire!

MY DANGEROUS DAUGHTER CHARLOTTE

Charlotte was called dangerous in her RS lesson today,
The reason was she had a knife, according to her TA.

Lies, replied Charlotte as she went upon her way,
And reported it to her parents when she got home that day.

It will be looked into, said the Assistant Principal, I will find
out what went on, and then will let you know.

Her parents would be contacted, with the story of the truth,
But when the telephone did ring, they darn near hit the roof.

I have now taken a statement of what went on that day, I will
read it to you, what the TA had to say.

"I didn't say a thing, everything was of the norm, if you want
to find a culprit, I would just blame her friend Storm".

WHERE'S ME TENT

Well, I pitched me tent,
Then went out for the day,
But the wind it came up,
And blew it away.

When I came back,
From a lovely day,
I couldn't find me tent,
It had blown right away.

Though I still had the frame,
It was buckled and bent,
can't find me tent,
Don't know where it went.

The wind it died down,
And at least it was dry,
So I slept in the car,
But I wanted to cry.

Early next day,
couldn't take anymore,
So I packed up me car,
Could be back home by four.

As with the wind,
My camping did hamper.
I'll come back next year,
This time with a camper!

MY HERO

I wrote these poems, whilst sitting upstairs.
To be like my hero,
Whose name is Pam Ayres.

She has a talent, I'm sure you'd agree,
I just like to hope, you think the same about me!

MY LITTLE CAR IS PAST IT!

My little car is past it,
It's time to say Goodbye.
We've been together for ten years,
I think I'm gonna cry.

We have travelled several miles,
We did it every day.
From primary school to college,
'Til the children moved away.

Now I have to trade you in,
And get something quite new,
I no longer drive my little car,
Of rust and navy blue.

Faults, you have so many,
I must admit that's true.
But you see, I loved that car,
Which once was navy blue.

I'm not the only sad one,
To know that you're not there.
At the ending of your motoring life,
It's you I had to share.

With the Breakdown Co, and garage,
Who worked hard to repair you,
And a trip to the breakers yard,
Was something I could spare you.

Sadly, that time has now come,
The clock it loudly ticks,
As you have gone beyond repair,
The garage it can't fix.

I drive you one final time,
And think of all we've done,
So thank you to my little car,
We had a lot of fun.

MY PASSPORT NEEDS RENEWING

Well, I wanted to renew my passport,
so I could go away.
There's still some foreign places,
where I would like to stay.

But first I need a photo,
so I had to make a move,
And off I went to get it done,
in a photo booth.

Well, you'd think it would be simple,
just sit and look and grin,
But remember who you're talking about,
and so when I went in…

I had to sit upon a seat,
it really was a must,
But the flipping thing, it would not move,
And I needed it to adjust!

Once I finally managed that,
the camera with its flashes,
Meant then that, I couldn't see at all,
as I'd taken off me glasses.

Well, the sun it had caught my face,
I saw as I had a gander,
So when photo number one came out,
I looked just like a panda.

Surely photo number two,
Would really look the max,
But I nearly died of shock,
Who is that battle axe!

Finally, photo number three,
I chose that one at random,
It wasn't any better,
To the passport office I had 'em.

Well, that photo must have caused a hoot,
Amongst the passport staff,
'cos the letter with my passport read,
Thanks for giving us a laugh!

NOSEY NEIGHBOUR

We have a nosey neighbour,
Who lives half way down our street,
He has to know what's going on,
And never is discrete.

He interrogates the neighbours,
And new people he does meet,
He just has to know the business,
Of anyone in our street.

What number have you moved in to,
And, how much did you pay,
I've lived in this street, for several years,
I'll never move away.

So now he has a nickname,
We smile, our lips are curled,
Look out, here he comes again,
Our own News of the world!

ODE TO A LAND ROVER

I wanted something bigger, than the little car we had,
To tow my larger caravan, which made my car feel bad.
I wanted an estate car, but thought that it's too big,
Besides a car more suited, would make a better rig.

So through an auto magazine, the pages I do flick,
And looking at these prices, it made me feel quite sick.
But did my eyes deceive me, I look again and see,
Ah, now I know just what I want, a Land Rover's for me.

I look at all the old ones, yes some are in my price,
If only I can get one, that cream one looks quite nice.
So off we go to see it, my wife she likes it too,
We come home with our "new" car, built in seventy-two.

But pretty soon the problems, come on in leaps and bounds,
The rain it leaks in everywhere, and what's that funny sound.
They say a Land Rover owner, he doesn't wander far, and
When at last you see him 'Tis underneath his car.

Oh Landie we do love you, with all your power and mite,
But not so dear old Landie, when you're not running right.

OFF TO DARTMOOR

It was Christmas Day on Dartmoor,
Cold but bright with sun,
So lots of fed up people,
Went out there for a run.

Kids with new mountain bikes,
Riding on the grass,
whilst lots of people walking dogs,
Gathered there on mass.

Teenagers with new smart phones,
iPads and MP3 players,
older people feeling cold,
wearing coats with lots of layers.

No one really wanted,
to stay home and watch T.V.
Full of boring programs,
which they didn't want to see.

So we're all off to Dartmoor,
To walk up on the Tors,
All dressed up like Eskimos,
To walk across the moors.

OFF TO UNI (A LITTLE MESSAGE FOR MUM)

I'm off to university,
I hope it will be fun,
Don't worry, I'll be back again,
with the washing for me mum!

OH DEER IT'S MARK

Driving in my new car, I really did feel proud,
Until along a stretch of road, there came a bang quite loud.

I looked out through my mirror, my eyes were full of fear,
As laying on the roadside, was a very large old deer.

The poor thing was no longer, and when at last I stop.
I open up my car door, and out I quickly hop.

I look around in horror, at my pride and joy,
That deer has really done for it; it's crumpled like a toy.

And so a word of warning, out walking light or dark,
if you are a deer or such, keep out the way of MARK!

OH HECK - ME BRAKES HAVE FAILED

Well, I was driving along in me car, when the warning lights came on,
I was wondering why this happened, whatever had gone wrong.
I'd driven to the college, to drop me son off like you do,
Then going to the school, to drop my daughter off there too.

But my car it had decided, it was gonna make us late,
And when I turned the corner, out of the college gate…
I realised what the warning was, it gave me quite a shock,
As putting on my brakes, the car it would not stop.

It would have been quite simple, it made me feel quite ill,
'cos me brakes when they had failed, was at the top of a ruddy hill.
I managed very slowly, using handbrake to stop,
Thankfully not at the bottom of it, but at the very top.

That's when I heard my daughter's voice,
Saying in my ear, what do you think you're doing Mum,
We cannot park out here.

I was so surprised to hear her,
Sitting there on her own,
With earphones stuck into her ears,
Listening to her I-phone.

She doesn't usually say a word,

She doesn't hear a sound,
Just sits there with earphones on,
With music all around.

But…

She took them off to listen,
As I told her of our fate.
She replied, please don't stop here Mum,
Or you're gonna make me late!

OLD FLAME I DON'T THINK SO

I've tried to tell you nicely,
But it just don't seem to work.
Please will you go away from me?
You really are a burke.

Your chat up lines are boring,
You're not every woman's dream.
More like a nightmare,
You make me wanna scream.

I can't stand the sight of you,
I'm sorry it's no joke.
You really are a prize twit,
A really silly bloke.

How many times must I tell you?
Why don't you go away?
I do not want to be your friend,
That's all I have to say.

I don't want to know you,
I've tried to make it plain,
When we went out on our first date,
Said, I don't want to see you again.

So just for old times' sake,
I'll tell you once again,
You weren't even a flicker,
Let alone a dear old flame!

AN EXPENSIVE WALK

Out on the moors we went for some fun,
Let off the Greyhound, so he had a run.

The wind it was blowing, into his face,
And being ex racer, he wanted to race.

As he got faster and turned rather steep,
Then out of nowhere, there appeared two sheep.

Amongst the rocks, they decided to wallow,
And our silly Greyhound, decided to follow.

The sheep then ran off, it wasn't a joke,
As caught in the rocks, our Greyhound's foot broke.

The damage he did, was quite extensive,
And our little walk, turned out quite expensive!

ONLY A DOG

He was only a dog, that's what they said,
Only a dog, and now that he's dead.

Why do you grieve so, why do you cry?
He was only a dog, and you said your Goodbye.

Only a dog, but right to the end,
My constant companion, and dearly loved friend.

A friend ever faithful, a friend ever true,
And he didn't judge me, the way that you do.

And if I should cry, and if I should weep,
For my best friend, who I couldn't keep.

Please try to understand, and please try to see,
"Only a dog," he wasn't to me.

OUCH ME HEAD

I'm sorry, I know I shouldn't laugh,
I know that you are drunk,
But when you stuck your head down the loo,
And the seat hit it with a clunk.

I shouldn't laugh, I know it,
As you were being ill,
You had really drunk so much,
You had had your fill.

You looked so funny kneeling there,
With the seat upon your head,
And although it seemed to startle you,
Ouch, is all you said.

I'm sorry that I giggled so,
But you look so very daft,
It's made me really helpless,
As all I can do is laugh!

OUR PUPPY

Our puppy is a sweetheart,
You really want to see,
We only have one problem,
And that is all the pee.

He pees out in the garden,
But then he still has more,
And when you call him to you,
He pees upon the floor.

He pees when he's excited,
He pees when he's alone,
He pees upon your legs and shoes,
When he welcomes you back home.

He pees when he is running,
He pees when he's at play,
He pees upon his bedding,
And where he's gonna lay!

He pees when you pick him up,
And when you put him down,
He pees if you sit with him,
He pees upon the ground.

We think we'll have to change his name,
To little pee wee pup.
Or hope he will grow out of it,
Once he is grown up!

OUR PUPPY LOKI

Our little puppy, so cute and so sweet,
His head is too big, and so is his feet.

With his friend Zac, he just loves to play,
Chasing their toys in the garden at day.

It's in the mud where you love to dig,
And soon little puppy, you'll grown up and be big.

At last when it's bedtime, in his basket he'll creep,
And lay on his back, then fall fast asleep.

OUR ZAC

The German Shepherd sits tall and proud,
He's brave and loyal, with a bark so loud.

A beautiful dog, with fur so black,
That's our dog, whose name is ZAC.

PLEASE CAN I HAVE MY BABY BACK

Please can I have my baby back,
When he began to cry,
I threw him up into the air,
But I threw him way too high.

Well, we were in the garden,
And I didn't think at all,
When I seemed to have thrown him sideways,
And he went over my neighbour's wall.

Please can I have my baby back,
I'm glad that you were there,
As you then caught my baby,
As he flew up in the air.

Please can I have my baby back,
I know that it sounds bad,
But I was only playing with him,
Because I am his dad.

PLEASE TELL ME GOODBYE

I sit at the table, and give out a sigh,
Gazing at you, makes me wanna cry.
Why can't you say it, and just go oh why,
Just one little word, please tell me **Goodbye.**

I've given you hints, I've asked you to go,
Your brain's not too fast, in fact it's quite slow.
Having you with me would be less a tie,
If only you'd leave me, please tell me **Goodbye.**

But sadly it seems, that I'm not getting through,
I tried moving house, but then you moved here too.
I've tried saying **push off**, I can't tell a lie,
Oh if only you'd say it, please tell me **Goodbye.**

And now on my birthday, I so wanna cry,
you're still here with me, I ask myself **"WHY?"**
You'd make me so happy, if only you'd try,
with one little word, please tell me **Goodbye.**

POOR DOG

The vet did make a bad mistake,
He jabbed my dog and made him ache.

My dog he had to have an 'op,
And on three legs, he did hop.

It caused a swelling, in his thigh,
And pain so bad, it made him cry.

What he did, we couldn't tell,
So saw a new Vet, who made him well.

With so many pills to put him right,
My dog now does a rattle at night!

PUTTING UP THE AWNING

Well, I turned up with me caravan, to stay here on this site,
I then set up my caravan, in the early morning light.

I arrived here quite early, and as it is still morning,
Decided that I'd get to work, putting up the awning.

So I emptied out the awning bag, the awning and the poles,
Now to erect it, I try sorting out the poles.

But, looking at the poles, on the grass I fear,
That I forgot to mark them all, when I took them down last
year.

As I look on in bewilderment, I'm sure I'd got it right,
But the awning seems lopsided, the whole thing seems too
tight.

So I take it all down again, and have another try,
I'm sure that pole should go there, but this time it's too high.

And so I take it down again, I'll just have one last go,
but this time as I get it right, a gale force wind does blow.

The awning it does flap about, just like a giant kite,
Now the family join me, holding on with all their might.

Thank goodness it's all done now, my awning looks the best,
Unlike me, I'm shattered, I think I need a rest!

RAIN

When I hang out my washing,
In the blazing sun,
The sky turns black,
It starts to rain,
It really isn't fun.

I like to hang my washing out,
But I can make a bet,
That when I bring it in again,
My washing's sopping wet.

My neighbours hang their washing out,
On their washing line,
And when they do, it will be dry,
As the weather it stays fine.

But me, I'm just unlucky,
It really is a pain,
Each time I hang my washing out,
Then it will start to rain.

SANTA'S JOKE

In amongst the ferns and holly,
Santa left this ugly dolly.

So dear Santa with your sack,
Please will you come and take her back.

This dolly that is so new,
Talks as if she has the flu.

She's laying there upon my bed,
With yellow hair upon her head.

So now that you have had your joke,
I know you are a real nice bloke.

Please dear Santa, bring your sleigh,
And take this awful gift away!

SCARY!

If I'm not back within the hour,
Call in the S.A.S.
As I enter the small dark room,
It's really quite a mess!

I trip and I stumble,
It really is quite scary,
And I give out a little scream,
As I touch something hairy!

I find remains of rotten food,
And empty cans of drink,
'Why did I come into this room?'
I then begin to think.

At last I find the switch,
And quietly turn on the light,
I can't believe my eyes,
As I gaze upon the sight.

I know you're in here somewhere,
In the dark and gloom,
It really is quite scary,
Entering a teenager's room!

SID THE SPIDER

Sid the spider, hung from a thread,
He's just been e-mailing,
His old mate Fred.

I know that spiders, can give you a fright,
But Sid the spider he's alright,
As he even has his own web site.

THAT RUDDY G.P.S

I decided to use my G.P.S as I was going somewhere new,
I didn't know how to get there; I didn't have a clue.

So, I entered all the info, I didn't get it wrong,
I thought it would be easy, as I slowly drove along.

I followed the directions, at the next exit, you go straight,
I thought it seemed a little odd, as I drove through an open
gate.

But I followed the directions, and my fate was quickly sealed,
I wasn't on the motorway, but in a muddy field.

Well, I finally reached my destination, although it was quite
late,
my little car was muddy, and with a G.P.S I hate.

Now, making a mistake, isn't such a sin,
But I grabbed that ruddy G.P.S, and threw it in the bin!

THE BEACH WALK

Walking on a sandy beach,
With my dogs playing ball,
I slipped upon a muddy patch,
And promptly I did fall.

When I had slipped over,
I landed with a thud,
And when I got back up again,
I was covered in wet mud.

My husband and my sister,
Walking that way too,
Doubled up with laughter,
At what I did just do.

You'd think that I'd get questioned,
As to whether I'm alright.
But every time they looked at me,
They laughed at such a sight.

So off we went to find the car,
Making our way back,
When my Husband turned to me and said,
You can't get in like that.

You're not going to sit on my seats,
As I won't have a muddy patch,
So instead, you'll have to travel,
With the dogs inside the hatch.

THE BROKEN DOWN LAND ROVER

Oh dear, I think my car is ill,
I went to drive it up the hill,
But before we reached the top,
My old Land Rover it did stop.

I'm late for work, I can't go home,
Thank goodness for that nearby phone.
I ring for help, please come quick,
We just can't move, the motors sick.

I know that I am in the way,
I hope I'm not stuck here all day,
I cannot push, and cannot pull,
My old Land Rover who will not go.

The man arrives to have a look,
He doesn't have a breakdown truck,
Says, I know it will, I know I can,
Pull you up with my small van.

I look at him in dumb surprise,
I still cannot believe my eyes,
Is he really such a dope?
Attached to us, with his tow rope.

Into his van, he jumps at will,
To tow us up that blooming hill,
But my faith in him does lack,

As its us who pulls him back.

As the smoke flies from his van,
To tow us up, still thinks he can,
When at last he does give up,
And from his smoking van, does hop.

The problem now, he starts to think,
Yes, I know, it needs a drink.
So off he goes with some cash,
To buy my Landie, some more gas.

So with gladness in my heart,
I wave Goodbye, as we do part.
At last I'm off to work you see,
My happy old Land Rover and me.

THE CAT

They say the cat has nine lives,
It's really just as well,
As from a second floor window,
This cat just went and fell.

It looked so stunned and frightened,
As it fell upon its feet,
It gave me the impression,
That it must have been asleep.

Falling from the window sill,
It won't do that no more,
'cos when I saw that cat again,
'twas sleeping on the floor.

THE COMPANY MAN

The company man, he has a big plan,
to take on more and more Staff.
He's not very wise so he chooses the guys,
He sees as his very close friends.

And now you can see, that this big company,
Pretty soon it will go to the wall,
As he's made them all bosses,
Now they have big losses,
As they haven't no workers at all!

THE DIRTY DOG

After a walk in the woods for an hour,
Our dog he was filthy, and needed a shower.

Well, GSD's love water, in books it's said,
But sadly these books, our dog he hasn't read.

He hates getting wet, won't go out in the rain,
don't mention a bath, or he goes quite insane.

He's dirty and smelly, but you're having a laugh,
If you think you are getting him into the bath.

Time it ticks by hour after hour, and still we can't get,
Him, into the shower.

At least it is Summer, and so we suppose,
We'll take him in the garden, then spray him with the hose!

THE DOG'S THOUGHTS

I am a dog, and if I could but talk,
I'd like to tell you, that I want a walk.

I'd go to a place with lots of green space,
Then I could chase rabbits all over the place.

And I'd chase a stick or give you a lick,
'cos if I'm chasing rabbits, I have to be quick.

Although, it's not fun, when fast they do run,
And they're faster and quicker than me.

But then in the wet, you can surely bet,
It's puddles and mud that I see.

I'll have so much fun, as I jump in each one,
And soon you won't recognize me.

Then after an hour, you'll take me home for a shower,
And I'll look so clean and so neat.

But you can be sure, once you open that door,
Out in the garden you'll see.

That out in the mud, I'll lie down with a thud,
Dirty and muddy, that's me!

THE DRUNK

The drunk he stumbled up the steps,
He really was quite dense,
As he caught hold of a hanging wire,
And fell back through the fence.

He really looked quite startled,
As he sat there with a frown,
He thought he'd reached the top step,
Not fallen right back down.

I just could not believe it,
As he had another try,
And did the same thing as before,
He looked like he would cry.

He sat there for a moment,
And then gave out a laugh,
This time he didn't use the steps,
He crawled along the path!

THERE'S SLUGS IN ME GARDEN

Well, I got slugs in me garden,
They're eating all me greens,
I've tried getting rid of them,
But even more I've seen.

The slug pellets, they are useless,
I put them out each day,
The ruddy slugs just love 'em,
Will they ever go away?

A friend then she suggested,
Instead I try some beer,
Apparently when they drink it,
They come over all quite queer.

Now, I don't know about you,
But I really draw the line,
A beer garden for slugs and snails?
In your garden, not in mine.

It conjures up weird visions,
Of them sitting at a bar,
Or singing rowdy songs,
Even playing a guitar.

But what really happens,
Once they've had a drink,
They slip off the cabbage leaves,
And drown there in the sink!

THE EXAM

Well my Niece she had an exam, but she was feeling rather ill,
The teacher said, no matter, she'd have to do it still.

And so the exam staff didn't know what to do, as she had to
leave the class room, and was sick out in the loo.

When she felt a little better, and she was on the mend,
She was seated at a desk, on the very end.

Sitting her exam, she didn't want to muck it,
So sat there at her end desk, and the Staff gave her a bucket!

THE FAULTY CAR ALARM

Well, I brought me car home from shopping, and parked it like before. Hit the alarm remote button. So that it would lock the door.

But once the door had locked, and I went to walk away,
The alarm, it then decided that it would have a play.

So it then disarmed itself, and opened up the door,
When I alarmed it once again, the door unlocked once more!

I was getting rather desperate, so I locked it with the key,
Then turned to go into my house, can't believe what I did see...

The car doors had unlocked again, the alarm started to bleep,
Then the lights began to flash, as to my house I creep.

So, back to my car I go, and lock it with the key, but still the doors unlock again, as I begin to flee.

I rush back to my house, and make a hasty retreat, didn't lock the doors this time, 'cos I know when I am beat.

An appointment with the garage, I do make the next day,
But by now the battery's flat, so my car is towed away.

Expected that the garage, had now put it right, they'd taken in my car and kept it overnight.

To my surprise they told me, they could not find a fault, the alarm caused them no problems, but it gave my pride a jolt!

So once again it's back with me, my car outside my door,
No flashing lights or bleeping sounds, as my alarm it works no more!

THE FEMALE DRUNK

The drunk she sat upon her wall,
A dog between her feet,
She glares and swears at everyone,
Walking past her in the street.

She sits there during summertime,
With a cup filled up with drink,
She really is quite beautiful,
Or so she seems to think.

She eyes up all the passing men,
And dazzles them with her smile,
But as her teeth are rotten,
You can see they run a mile.

DEDICATED TO JACKS BRANCH
FREDDIE – OUR GREYHOUND
2003 to 2008

I ran so many races,
I really was the best,
Then I started losing,
So I was made to rest.

No more the useful item,
Making lots of cash,
Taken to a rescue centre,
Got rid of in a flash.

I wasn't very lucky,
As no one wanted me,
People wanted puppies,
Not a dog of three.

Moved on to another centre,
And there I had some luck,
Some people really liked me,
And to their home I'm took.

Now I have an owner,
I'm part of a family,
No longer someone's item,
I'm loved because I'm me.

THE GUY SINGING TWO FIELDS AWAY

Please can someone shut him up,
That guy thinks he can sing,
The noise he makes is very loud,
Now I can't hear a thing.

He started 'bout an hour ago,
The mike he had a took it,
But he can't hold a flipping note,
Not even in a bucket!

Now as we were camping,
And had started to pack up,
that's when we heard, that awful din,
Kept hoping he would stop.

At last his song has ended,
He had a good long run,
Oh no, I can't believe it,
He's started another one.

Can't someone take the mike from him,
Or turn the darn thing down,
Looks like he's driving the locals,
Quickly out of town.

When he had finally finished,
The crowd they gave a clap,
Not 'cos he's got talent,
Just glad he won't be back.

THE HEDGEHOG

Normally they are quite shy,
Hiding from all passersby,
But when it's late and shadows fall,
Amongst the shadows on the wall.
If you're quiet, you will see,
A hedgehog and her family.

Mum and babies tiptoe by,
Guided by a moonlit sky,
Out there for to find their tea,
There's milk for you, and bread for me.
Kindly Humans, caring souls,
Left it there in little bowls.

And now as daylight fills the sky,
They hurry off without Goodbye,
To find a place so safe and deep,
Then curl up tight, and go to sleep.

THE DOG

I sit alone and wonder why,
My owner's gone, it makes me cry.
Oh why, oh why, did she leave me,
Without even a bone for tea.

I pace and dig, and dig and pace,
I have to get out of this lonely place.
I bark and howl, and scratch and chew,
Is this what I'm meant to do.

The time drags by, I'm so alone,
I only want a loving home.
Instead I sit here full of woe,
Why she left I'll never know.

But wait, is that a noise I hear,
I turn my head and lift my ear.
Oh joy, it is, I've company,
As in the lock there turns a key.

Oh you are a naughty pup,
You've torn the mat, and chewed it up.
You've made such noises, I don't know,
I just went out, and you couldn't go.

It's alright I bark with glee,
My mistress hasn't deserted me,
I know I really shouldn't moan,
As I was only left at home.

THE OWL

It was a dark and moonless night,
The owl he gazed upon the sight.
For there was a mouse for tea,
That only this barn owl could see.

In noiseless flight it made its dare,
And swooped down low from in the air.
All went silent, night held its breath,
As that poor mouse he met his death.

Happy now that he'd had his tea,
Away he flew so silently.
And as the world began to wake,
Off to his bed, that owl did make.

THE PASSING OF NORMAN THE GOLDFISH

Norman the goldfish,
Has sadly passed away,
He was quite old for a goldfish,
We buried him today.

THE PLOT

The dog it sat upon the stair,
Gave out a growl, there's someone there.

So to the door, I did trot,
I didn't know, it was a plot.

Promising himself a treat,
My sausage rolls that dog did eat.

No one calling at the door,
Just sausage roll crumbs on the floor.

THE PUPPY IN THE BATH

My puppy likes the bathroom, he likes to see the bath,
And all the water in it, he really is a laugh.

So when the room was open, with the water pouring there,
He left what he was doing, and tore upon the stair.

Then right into the bathroom, this pup of mine he crept,
And straight into the bathtub, he only went and leapt.

He tried to grab the bubbles, floating in the tub,
And against the flannel that puppy he did rub.

And so now in the future, we'll have to shut the dog,
As my puppy left huge puddles upon the bathroom floor.

THE RETIREMENT POEM

I'm running out of ideas,
I don't know what to write,
I've been sitting here for ages,
Looks like it'll take all night.

I'm supposed to write a poem,
For someone who's just retired,
But by the time, I've made one up,
He'll probably have expired!

THE ROBIN

A little Robin redbreast, sat upon my tree,
He sat there swinging on a branch,
Just waiting for his tea.

It was a cold dark winter's day,
And snow lay all around,
Not a scrap of food to eat,
Down there on the ground.

I put out nuts and water,
Bread and birdie treat,
And upon my bird table,
That Robin he did eat.

When he ate his fill,
And off to find his bed,
He sat upon my windowsill,
With pretty breast of red.

Now with thank you's over,
It was time to go,
Now that he was warm,
And his small tum it was full.

THE SCHOOL RUN

Come on, it's eight fifteen,
We're already running late,
James you're not even dressed yet,
And we should have left at eight.

How do I know where you left your shoes?
Where did you last discard them?
I saw the dog run off with something,
maybe they're in the garden.

Charlotte, you've not got your tie,
You can't have lost them all,
Maybe when you took it off last night,
You filed it on the floor.

What's the hold up this time James?
Can't find your college pass,
So back into the bedroom,
We madly make a dash.

It's in your bedroom somewhere,
don't stand there looking dumb.
If you leave it long enough,
It'll always be found by Mum.

Can we please depart now?
The dogs are stood by me,
What's the matter Charlotte?
You forgot, you have PE.

We'll wait for you in the car then,
Please try to hurry up.
Good, now have you both got everything?
'Cos I'm not gonna stop.

At last, we now have dropped James off,
I just have to drive around,
Now, where do I drop you Charlotte?
No answer, she's wired for sound.

I'm nearing the bus bay now,
Do you want dropping there,
Or in the school's drop off point?
But you just sit and stare.

Did you say something Mum?
I don't know what you said,
I had my earphones on again,
Listening to music instead.

See you later I call, as I go to drive away,
Off on to the moors now,
It's a lovely sunny day.

I don't believe it Charlotte,
You had it on your back,
I clearly saw you with it,
When you left the house with Zac.

So you want me to go back home,
I don't really want to nag,
But I can't understand it,
How you forgot your bag!

THE WASHING MACHINE

It's time that my washing machine retired,
It's worked hard in its life, and has now expired.

Brought in a replacement, a newer design,
And for a while, the machine it worked fine.

After a month, things weren't so good,
My machine wasn't working, the way that it should.

The repair man came out, time after time,
And the neighbours now think, this is his house,
not mine.

Even the shop, just couldn't keep pace,
So another machine, delivered in its place.

At last, a machine that is working just fine,
And a lot of clean clothes, flap out on the line.

But… just a month later, my machine goes off **BANG**,
And the whole ruddy saga, starts over again!

THERE'S A RAT IN ME OUTHOUSE!

There's a rat in me outhouse, it gave me such a fright.
I was packing up me BBQ, 'cos we had lost the light.

I'd opened the outside toilet, just like I always do,
That's when I saw this blooming rat, a sitting on me loo.

I swore rather loudly, as I came upon the scene,
My wife she didn't see it, good job or she would scream.

And as it scurried off, this creature oh so black,
I'm sure I heard it mumble, don't worry, I'll be back!

THOSE BLINKING CHRISTMAS LIGHTS

The Christmas lights inside the house,
Sparkle there so bright,
And so I took some outside,
To brighten up the night.

It took me such a long time,
To hang them out just right,
But when I tried to turn them on,
I find that they won't light.

I really wouldn't have minded,
If there was just a few,
But if I have to test them all,
There's hundreds I must do.

I stand there in the freezing cold,
With patience I do lack,
I cannot feel my fingers,
And the sky now has turned black.

I stand there in the pouring rain,
Decide then to go in,
And rip those flipping lights down,
And bung them in the bin.

THOUGHTS OF OUR GERMAN SHEPHERD AT THE VETS!

You won't get me in there Mum,
You can start taking bets,
You won't get me in that little room,
'cos I knows, it is the vets.

You got me in there first time Mum,
But that was just a trick,
You won't get me in there again,
Even if I'm sick.

I know I'm GSD Mum,
And that I'm brave and proud,
But I will not go in there Mum,
I'll just whine and bark so loud.

I know I see the vet Mum,
For my yearly jab,
But I don't really want it,
Just give it to that Lab'

I'm not going in that room Mum,
You can drag me along the floor,
But you're still going to have a problem Mum,
I'm not going through that door!

And when it's time to enter Mum,
And the nurse calls out my name,
I'll certainly not be going in there,
'cos I'll cling on to the door frame!

THOUGHTS OF AN OLD AGED POP STAR

Well, I'm a famous singer, as well you all do know,
And all over the world each year, on tours I like to go.

But as I'm getting older, me body it starts ailing,
Me hearing it is going, and me eyesight it is failing.

Me back it keeps aching, it goes out more than me,
And out there on the stage at night, I can hardly see.

Tonight though I am puzzled, I don't know what went wrong,
It must have been my ruddy band, that got the keys all wrong!

I used to go out on the stage, and sing for an hour or two,
But now I have to cut it short, as I keep needing the loo.

I'd party late into the night, with girls with hair of red,
But now when I come off the stage, I'm ready for me bed.

My fan mail that I used to get, saying it's me that they require,
Has certainly changed its tune now, all telling me RETIRE!

WE DON'T WANT OUR PHOTO TAKEN MUM

We don't want our photo taken Mum,
It really isn't fun,
You take so long to take the snap,
And you make us face the sun.

The sun it does near blind us,
And developing cost a mint,
The photos they are ruined,
As the sun has made us squint.

The way we stand and smile,
Has to be right for you,
It makes us so embarrassed,
As behind you forms a queue.

While Dad is stood impatiently,
He really wants to go,
Telling you to hurry up,
It's not a studio.

And looking at your snapshots Mum,
Not ruined by the sun,
Those are not good either,
As they're ruined by your thumb.

WHAT A RACKET

My neighbours keep their washing machine, outside in their shed,
It bangs and rattles when it's used, I think it'll soon be dead.

It sounds more like a lorry, going up a hill,
You cannot hear yourself think, it really sounds quite ill.

The worst part is the spin cycle, they should send for the menders,
If you go in the garden now, you need some ear defenders!

WHERE DID I PARK MY CAR

Well, I parked my car in Tesco,
And once in there I'd shopped.
When I came back out again,
Couldn't find where I'd stopped.

I look at all the parked cars,
Did I park over there?
I look upon my usual space,
But no, it isn't there.

I know I brought it with me,
I drove it here this morning,
Surely it couldn't disappear,
Not without a warning.

I'd alarmed it when I got out,
But where was that I fear,
I wish that I could find it,
Though sadly it's not here.

I'm starting now to panic,
I've walked the whole car park,
Ah ha I think I've found it,
As my dog he starts to bark.

When I'm finally leaving Tesco,
My dog gives out a little bark,
Meaning, when we come here next time,
Please remember where you park.

WHERE'S ME CHRISTMAS TURKEY

Oh where's me Christmas turkey,
I really need to know.
I left it on the kitchen shelf,
With me oven set on low.

I was sitting in the front room,
Watching the T.V.
The bird had finished cooking,
So I made a cup of tea.

Now, I know it can't have wandered off,
I'm beginning to see red.
It would have been a miracle,
As the flipping thing is dead!

I storm around the kitchen,
I check out all the shelves,
Maybe it was Santa,
Who has took it for his elves.

And so back to the front room,
I go with aching head,
Thinking of my family,
Who no longer will get fed.

It's then I see my turkey,
Well, only what's left over.
'Cos laying in his basket,
Is a well fed dog called Rover!

WHY ARE MY TEENAGERS ALLERGIC TO THE BIN

Why are my teenagers, allergic to the bin?
I placed one in their bedroom, for their rubbish to go in.

But they seem quite unaware, of how to chuck things in,
So they throw it on the floor, and my patience's running thin.

They know how to play their music, on iPads and smart phone,
But binning all their rubbish, it really makes me moan.

As picking up their rubbish, that doesn't seem like fun,
So they throw it on the floor, and leave it there for Mum.

WRONG NUMBER

The phone it rang this morning,
So I got out of my bed,
"Hello, is that the doctors?"
A booming voice then said.

"No," I said, "you've got it wrong,"
And back to bed I lumber,
I'm getting sick and tired,
Of answering a wrong number.

The phone it rang yet once again,
I'm sick I have the flu,
The same voice is then off again,
Oh, flipping heck, not you.

I stare down at my telephone,
Is this somebody new,
But when I answer it once more,
Oh, flipping heck,
Not you.

This time as it rings yet again,
And from my bed I hop,
That's it, no more, I've had enough,
I'm going down the shop!